Puthalath Raghuprasad has many talents. His first talent is painting. His favorite medium is oil, and he creates realistic pictures on canvas, including portraits, scenery/landscapes, birds, animals, and flowers. His second talent is writing in prose, but lately, he has also written several poems. He is also proficient in inventing; he holds 21 US patents, and two of them are at different stages of manufacturing. Finally, he has formulated his own theory about the universe in which gravity and the ever-present axial rotation cooperate to give rise to the motions of all celestial bodies.

I dedicate this book to the memory of Rev. Fr. Reynolds, my English teacher at St. Joseph's College, Devagiri, Kozhikode, Kerala, India, who recognized my flair for writing in English and encouraged me to become a journalist. I also dedicate this book to my daughter, Chantel, a veterinarian who has truly devoted her life to the welfare of all animals.

Puthalath Raghuprasad

BROKEN TUSK

AUSTIN MACAULEY PUBLISHERS™

LONDON • CAMBRIDGE • NEW YORK • SHARJAH

This is a work of fiction. Names, characters, businesses, places, events, locales, and incidents are either the products of the author's imagination or used in a fictitious manner. Any resemblance to actual persons, living or dead, or actual events is purely coincidental.

Ordering Information
Quantity sales: Special discounts are available on quantity purchases by corporations, associations, and others. For details, contact the publisher at the address below.

Publisher's Cataloging-in-Publication data
Raghuprasad, Puthalath
Broken Tusk

ISBN 9781685621346 (Paperback)
ISBN 9781685621353 (Hardback)
ISBN 9781685621377 (ePub e-book)
ISBN 9781685621360 (Audiobook)

Library of Congress Control Number: 2023909537

www.austinmacauley.com/us

First Published 2023
Austin Macauley Publishers LLC
40 Wall Street 33rd Floor, Suite 3302
New York, NY 10005
USA

mail-usa@austinmacauley.com
+1 (646) 5125767

I offer my sincere gratitude to my friends and well-wishers who have encouraged me in writing this short novel. A special mention should be given to my son Saril's many suggestions, particularly his suggestion to add the last chapter, which, in retrospect, rounded off the story more satisfactorily.

Foreword

I was motivated to write this short novel by the plight of African elephants in the last half a century or so. These magnificent gentle giants roamed the great savannas of Africa for millions of years; as they are herbivores they did not come into conflict with other animals, and because of their size, they remained safe for much of their existence. This state of affairs changed in the last century, with the availability of high-power guns, equipped with telescopes and by the demand for their tusk for making and marketing mementos, as well as for their purported medicinal use in the East Asian countries. Such demand was compounded by the ease with which the poachers were able to cut into and extract the tusks by using the circular saw. Thus, the fate of these gentle giants was impacted, leading to the steady decline of their numbers.

Various governments and organizations have taken steps to reverse the course of this disastrous state of affairs, with only a limited degree of success. Banning the manufacture and sale of mementos made from elephant tusks and confiscating and destroying the stockpiles of elephant tusks have barely made a dent in this tragedy. The reason for this failure is, of course, the continued demand for elephant tusks for medicinal purposes, and the high price they fetched in the underground market. So, what is the solution? I came to the conclusion that educating the masses will be an essential component of this effort, and with the publishing of this short novel, drawing the attention of the masses to the plight of the elephants, I can make a small contribution. This novel is designed to educate the children, although many adults may also need such education. In addition, some consistent efforts at discouraging the use of elephant tusks for medicinal purposes need to be done; here, the respective governments have seminal roles. Their consumers should be made aware of the fact that the tusks have no medicinal value, but also legislation to ban such use must be enacted. Another, humane measure that can be done is to capture the elephants, cut their tusks short so that they are not targets of the poachers, and thus save them from the poachers' guns. This would be far more effective and productive than confiscating and destroying tusks after their owners have been butchered!

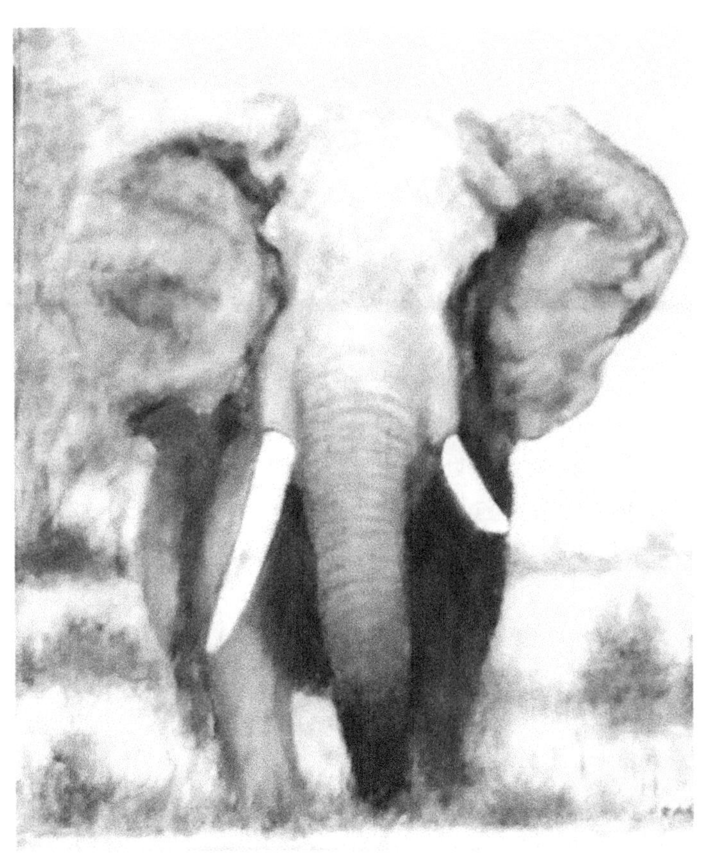

Hi! It's me, Broken Tusk!

Chapter One

"Mom! Broken tusk is bothering me," squealed "Baby." (I call him Trouble.)

He had his ears raised, the head shaking from side to side in fake distress and the tail raised.

He continued, "He is throwing stones at me."

That was so typical of him! All I had done was sprinkle some dusty soil on him, just for fun. And that translates to stone-throwing! His mother is my aunt. She is the elder female in our group and thus the chief (so to speak). We call her 'Spotty' as she had spots of light-colored skin around her neck. She looked at me sternly, as if to say, "Watch out," but this time she said nothing.

Baby

By now 'Trouble' was faking pain and was groaning. He was shaking his tail from side to side violently.

My aunt Spotty was nearby but again did not say or do anything. It looked as if she had left that job to another aunt, who came to investigate; no, to mediate. She was Aunt Smiley. She was not exactly an aunt but a big sister. But everyone called her aunt. She earned the adjective Smiley by her disposition, and she had come to live up to that.

She said, "Why are you creating trouble for us?"

"You got that one right. It's trouble who is creating it."

I glanced toward Baby. By now, he had his head down. No more complaining. He walked toward a group of juveniles a few paces away and that was that. Thus ended that crisis.

Ours was a herd of twenty-six. My home had everything I could hope for, with a large area in which to play and rummage. I had great company. There were fourteen other juveniles in our group. The days were occupied mostly by play. Sometimes we chased the pesky deer. Sometimes we just dug the ground with our feet. Now, that was fun. Kicking up the dust. Then throwing some of it on everyone around. We'd try to get the adults into this action. But more often than not they did not join in.

Some members of my beautiful family

I heard the familiar low-pitched call from Aunt Spotty (remember, my aunt who was the chief of our group?). She was asking the group to move to another location.

"Come on, everybody, what's the delay?" she asked.

Slowly everyone stopped what he or she was doing and started to follow her. By then, she had moved on fifty or so paces. She was followed closely by the less senior females and then the juniors. We tried to keep in line but when we didn't and the hierarchy was not followed, we knew we'd get punished. No one wanted to get a 'nudge' (it was more like a kick on the back leg and, I can assure you, it's no fun) from her or her lieutenants.

We weren't sure where she was taking us but no one had the guts to question her. She was at the front of the line, walking with authority, wagging her tail from side to side. A slow, measured pace. This may mean a show of authority but it could just be she was allowing all the kids to keep up with the group. I was in the middle of the herd. It was always fun to walk with all the members of the group as when we elephants walked, all the others gave way. Now, that was fun. There were no other animals that would challenge us. And that knowledge was quite reassuring.

My closest friend Rash adjusted his pace so he could come close to me. His name was most appropriate as he did things in a 'rash' way. His temperament and character suited me just fine and that was why we were best of friends. He asked me, sympathy obvious in his voice:

"That boy is a bit much isn't he?"

"Don't we all know?" I replied. "But he and all of us know his exalted position in this group. No escaping that."

"Just an accident of birth," said Rash. "But I hope I'll get a chance to get even one day."

We were walking quite fast now and beginning to pant.

"Do you have any idea where we are going? Spotty never tells us, does she?" I asked.

Rash agreed. "But, this route appears familiar. I think we've been through this route before."

"To where?"

"It's either to the river or to the spot where we dig for salt. Remember?"

"Huh. Oh, I guess. I am really tired."

"I wish Spotty would slow down. My legs are aching."

I was also aware of several pesky flies hovering around my ears. They didn't exactly bite but Oh! How annoying they were! I tried waving my ears wildly to get them to take off and preferably disappear. They did get startled and take off for short periods. But only for short periods; then, they come right back. They appeared to be bent on annoying me. No, that's not true. They were annoying everybody.

Thus, the long walk, the uncertainty of what was coming next, and the flies and birds that constantly accompanied us were taking a toll on all of us. But none of us had the courage to question Spotty; in the back of our minds was the realization that she was so experienced and full of knowledge that we could completely rely on her.

Thus we plodded on until we came upon a clearing that contained a sizable patch of water left from the last rainfall. Then we knew why they brought us here. That was where we dug and looked for mud. There was a definite technique in the process. Since we had come here and done these things before, I already knew the procedure. It was our (the juniors') job to educate the younger kids. I and the other juveniles ran ahead of the herd and jumped in. First, we had to find a site deep enough to remain partially submerged. In fact, this puddle was deep enough for the water level to touch my tummy. Umm! That felt nice.

After coming all that distance and the heat of the sun and then the gentle stroking by the edge of the water felt heavenly. We frolicked a bit and then started to dig deep into the riverbed. We had to first find the level, and then scrape to remove the top layer with our trunks. After that, we suck up the very soft mud and took some of it into our mouths. I don't know what the mud does but it always tasted quite good. Just like some of the leaves, with an earthy kind of taste. And the mud was soft and easy to swallow. It sure was fun. And I knew for sure it was good for us too. Why else would Spotty bring us here? She was very knowledgeable. We all trusted her experience and her knowledge and wisdom.

Spotty let all of us have plenty of time to dig and eat all the mud we wanted. Then it was time for throwing some of the mud on our bodies. This is another great treat we get from such mud holes. We'd stir up the mud, suck it up and then throw some of it over ourselves. We were forbidden to throw the mud around or on someone else. We must have been at the hole for a long time before Spotty motioned to us it was time to go. We followed the same process, kids protected by the grownups and the whole gang pacing back home. Only, all of us had a thick layer of mud on our skin and after it dried up, we looked distinctly healthier. We felt healthier too, with fewer parasites on the skin to contend with. Parasites such as ticks.

Soon we were heading back home. Our skins had cooled down from the water and, especially from the mud.

Chapter Two

Our life followed a fairly regular rhythm. A lot of time was spent in eating, which of course was most enjoyable. As soon as we were old enough to find our own food our elders let us forage. Although never far away from the group, we would eat the shrubbery and accessible leaves and small branches from the smaller trees. In some seasons, we also got a harvest of sweet fruits that fell to the ground from large trees. That was always a feast! The texture, the sweetness, and the certain aroma of the fruits! We would gobble up mouthfuls when they were plenty. When the season ended and the numbers of the fruits dwindled, we would pick individual ones and savor. There was no sharing for the most part, but there were no fights either. We just ate what we were able to pick up. Then, when the season was over, we looked forward to the next year's bounty.

When we weren't foraging for leaves, we were into just playing games. One of my favorite games was called 'tree-felling'. I liked it because it told you who was stronger and it was just clean fun. The game was played by the stronger juveniles. You push hard with your head and trunk on the trees and shake them. Shake, shake, shake until they keeled over and fell. Sometimes, when the game was over, many small trees would have fallen. Of course, one delightful consequence of this game was that all of us got to eat, lots of leaves once the tree had fallen. Some of us were really tired by the end of the games and they lie down to take a rest and doze off. Now, that was luxury!

Sometimes a terrible accident would happen to break up the fun-filled carefree life. Like the time when one day we were at the water-drinking place. The whole group was led by Spotty to this place and one by one all in our group were enjoying the cold water. We could drink and quench our thirst, but we would also squirt a good bit of the water over our heads and bodies to cool off. Our frolicking came to an abrupt halt when a beast with a long mouth and a long raw of strong, sharp teeth grabbed Perky's leg. He was called Perky because he was always ready to do anything. In fact, he reveled in trying new things. He was such a joy to be around! So, when this happened to Perky, everyone was concerned. All the grown-ups charged toward the site. Smarty, a grown-up aunt was the first to reach the place. She grabbed the beast by its tail and tried to throw it off. But, she couldn't extricate the beast from its grip on Perky's leg. And each attempt of Smarty only plunged Perky into more agony. He was trumpeting desperately by now. The beast was so strong, it managed to pull Perky deeper into the water. That was scary. We could see blood making the water nearby distinctly red.

All the juveniles and children ran out of the water and onto the land and safety—minus Perky, of course. Now Spotty came to the rescue. She quickly analyzed the problem and came up with another solution. And it turned out to be the right one and it spared Perky's life. She stomped on the beast's stomach with her right foot. And she repeated to stomp until the beast let go of Perky's leg. We could see that the beast was badly injured and might even go off to its death. Good riddance!

Perky's leg was also badly injured. It was bleeding profusely and Perky was limping badly. The elders gathered around him, feeling with their trunks and in general showing concern. The care shown by our folks was unique in that they left the tasks at hand and gathered around and made gestures that were instantly comforting to the sick and injured. Just the show of caring did a whole lot of good. With such care, the physical trauma took only a few days to recover from but the emotional trauma lasted forever.

Sometimes danger came not from strangers but from villains in our own midst. And of all the villains, 'Terror' was number one. He was the lone male, the so-called patriarch of the group. We were all terrified of him, even when he was in a good mood; and he was almost always in a bad mood. And also because he was so big and strong and had the longest tusks. He also had the worst temper. He didn't need much provocation to attack. And when he attacked, it spelled disaster for the victims. No one could even come close to challenging him. And sometimes we've seen Terror in a state of constant sexual excitement and running around like a mad elephant. This could go on for several days or weeks. I had seen him ooze a liquid from both sides of his head during those spells. While we were all terrified, we would look through the corners of ours eyes to gaze at him but ever so cautiously, in order not to evoke his ire. We particularly liked to watch him run after one reluctant female after another until one eventually gave in.

He always felt he was the Lord over the whole female landscape and, more often than not, he would get his way in that land.

Terror

I had also seen him have huge fights with other males who challenged him. The challenger and he would charge toward each other. This would kick up the dust and shake the earth. Finally, the heads, trunks, and tusks collided. That would be like an explosion. All of us juveniles and even the grown-ups used to run and take cover. After several charging and posturing displays, always the other males would give up and run away, tails lifted up in the air, and running as fast as they could. Terror didn't follow the other males after that retreat. Then, after the mad behavior came to an end, Terror would once again retreat to his lonely life outside the herd. Then we all knew we would have peace for some time.

My most terrifying experience happened one night. The whole group was resting after a day of exhausting activities. It was a quiet night, almost dark except for the disk of bluish light in the sky. And most of us were enjoying the coolness of the night and the quiet. The only disturbance came from the pesky flies. This meant the tails and ears were in almost constant action.

Keen Eyes, the young male with exceptional powers of observation, alerted us saying, "Look at these ugly beasts! And they seem to be heading straight toward us. They couldn't possibly be after anything that we have."

I looked across where Keen Eyes was pointing. Almost as if in a nightmare, we saw the stealthy approach of ugly-looking beasts. They were several paces away, but we could tell they were coming straight toward us. There were almost thirty of them. They had rather small faces, shiny eyes and short ears, and downward sloping, thick necks. The body was neither that of cats nor dogs. Short tails with a bushy end completed this ugly animal's appearance. Not very appealing, I must admit.

Oh, those ugly animals!

I said, half-jokingly, "They are not the best-looking animals around."

"Yes, but they sure seem determined." That was Gentle, one of the young females in our group. "I am afraid. They have sharp teeth. So intimidating."

"But what can they possibly do to us?" As usual, that was a youngster, appropriately called Brave Lad. He should really be called Foolish Lad as he was always running into trouble mostly because he wanted to show all of us how brave he was. He continued, "Look at them, they are so small. And we are so much bigger and stronger."

One of our aunties interrupted him by saying, "But look at their number. As a pack they can attack any one of us and do some serious harm." This aunty was called 'Pretty'. All of us agreed that she had the best features of all of the females, best full ears, pretty petite tusks, and a nice body. Of course, all the males cherish the smooth, unspoiled ears of a full-grown female in our society. Also, the gently rounded forehead. Pretty had all the good features and she knew it.

She continued. "Our best bet is to remain together in a formation." "Now, kids, get inside. We will guard you."

We all knew that when the grown-ups suggest we go into that formation, the threat was real. And, as usual, we lost no time in getting inside of the defensive formation the adults formed. We youngsters usually felt so safe once that kind of formation was built.

The beasts started to circle our group. Then they were staring at each of us. We pretended to not appear frightened, although there was some trepidation in all of us youngsters. We also instinctively knew that showing fear would be dangerous, as such creatures would take advantage of such weaknesses.

Then suddenly one of the beasts made the most obnoxious sound. It was somewhat like the noise made by an ass, but louder, more malicious, and definitely scary. In fact, the noise made our blood 'curdle' so to speak. One of the youngsters in our group was startled by the noise and began to run. Immediately the beasts began running after it. The more the youngster (Fidgety) ran, the closer the beasts' ring became. Now everyone realized the danger Fidgety was in. He was hopelessly outnumbered and in mortal danger.

Two of our oldest females, Spotty and Fat trunk ran as quickly as they could toward Fidgety. With ears flying, trunks held high, and trumpeting hard, they must have surely instilled fear in the beasts. No! They didn't seem perturbed much at all!

Those beasts seemed determined, and they seemed to know all the tactics of intimidation. They were making weird noises. Grunts, groans, and even squeals. Oh! How ugly they looked! And they had this obnoxious smell! The pack formed a tight formation around Fidgety and two other children. The kids looked so scared!

This intimidation and stalking must have gone on for a long time and we were sort of waiting to see what other tactics the beasts might employ. Suddenly, one of the ugliest of the beasts lunged forwards and caught the right leg of Fidgety. It was shaking its head violently and at the same time, its vice-like grip was firmly planted on the leg.

We were afraid the leg would break. The bite appeared so strong!

"Kick him off, Fidgety." That was an amateurish suggestion from one of the youngsters. Of course, no amount of 'kicking' from Fidgety was going to dislodge the beast!

"No, no, no," cried Spotty. "Just hang on tight. We'll help you."

So saying, she lunged forward as if to strike the beast with her tusks. Although she was a female, Spotty had the best-formed tusks among us.

Spotty's trusted assistant Fat Trunk reached Fidgety and tried to nudge the beast off. By now, there were three more beasts biting into Fidgety and she was crying loudly. She was in pain and mortal fear. Her eyes were opened wide in terror and half rolled up. Her trunk was held up in the air and her tail was waving wildly.

Spotty next tried to free Fidgety from the grip of one of the beasts, by using her trunk. She pulled hard on the beast.

No use. The teeth were firmly planted. Next Spotty used her trunk to beat hard on the beast. She tried to beat it…harder, harder.

The beast squealed and veered off to the left. But, it did not let go of the bite.

Fidgety was getting weak. Soon some more adults joined in and quickly out-maneuvered if not out-numbered the beasts. Then, as quickly as it started, the danger was over. The beasts melted into the night. By the time the ordeal was over, all the youngsters were on edge, shaking like leaves. We all knew that the memories of this experience would last a lifetime!

Fidgety was in a pitiable condition. She was crying out loud, literally writhing in pain. Her right back leg was badly wounded and blood was pouring from it. All the aunts and many of her cousins surrounded her to comfort her. They had their trunks gently stroking Fidgety's face, the body, and especially the injured leg above where it must have been hurting badly. This profuse show of affection must have helped Fidgety forget some of her pain. But, we could all tell she was devastated not just by the pain but also by the intense fear from her experience. And to think that it had to happen to, of all elephants, Fidgety!

She tried to lie down but the pain was too much. She had to take the weight off that leg. She tried shaking it back and forth. That didn't do much good. She leaned against one of the adults for a while, with the right leg lifted up. Then she would lay it down. This sequence was repeated a countless number of times. Throughout that night the rest of the group went through the agony of Fidgety suffering intense pain and everyone offered comfort but were unable to really make an impact.

One of the grown-ups brought some leaves to apply to the wound but, Fidgety didn't want them to touch her wound. Then someone tried squirting water on the wound. It did help a little bit, in reducing pain but not for long. And the blood was still flowing. We could see Fidgety was becoming weak. And, after what appeared to be infinity, Fidgety dozed off. That brought some relief to the community. Soon the tired members all lay down to sleep as well. The adults of course took turns to stay up and keep an eye on Fidgety.

Chapter Three

The life in the group had been severely disturbed by what happened to Fidgety. And everyone joined in the effort to help her. Ever since that incident Fidgety didn't get up or walk and did not even show any interest in eating. Her mother was by her side all along. Trying to coax her to eat. She was listless. While the pain must have subsided somewhat, the wound was looking angry and yellow fluid was discharging from it. She wasn't moving that leg much.

A melancholy had descended on the whole group. Nobody was really in the mood to do anything. Even Spotty appeared to be in a deep depression. We had not seen her in that condition before. We were used to seeing her in charge and always in an assertive role. But she even appeared vulnerable.

Days went by and the condition of Fidgety was getting worse. She barely even moved and did not eat much food. Her mother and the aunts continued to try their best to make her eat. They brought the choicest leaves and fruits. But, they just lay there. She didn't touch any of them.

"Baby, why don't you try at least?" One of the aunts asked.

"These are the best we could find. You need the energy to recover."

Fidgety didn't move.

Another juvenile kneeled next to Fidgety and gently held her trunk in his own and stroked for a while. He said nothing but the moment was drenched in deep emotions.

Everyone understood that Fidgety's very survival now depended on recovering from the injury she sustained from the attack. The whole herd's activities were at a standstill. No one had the mood to go about their affairs.

Fidgety moved her head but only to turn it to the other side. Her eyes were moist and she was groaning again. Obviously, she was in pain again.

Her mother asked her, "Is there anything you want from us? Do you want a drink?"

Fidgety was quiet.

"How about this fruit?" She was showing a round, greenish-yellow fruit with a sweet aroma. At any other time, Fidgety would have jumped at the chance.

She did not say anything. Just a deep sigh escaped from her lips. One could see her lips flaring as if she were searching for air. Her wound was raw and it was oozing copious amounts of a slightly yellowish but clear liquid. As well, one could see the wound itself showing yellow color and it had a yellow thick material in the middle.

Some of the members helped control her pain again by pouring cold water over the wound and, they took turns to do that. This did bring some relief to her. Increasingly, however, her pain-free intervals were growing shorter. Her mother noticed that she was getting short of breath and puffing visibly. She was trembling all over. She was also foaming at her mouth. The whole group was in a state of shock. Nobody played or go very far from the group anymore. The gloom was all-pervasive.

This state of affairs went on for several more days. All the elders tried their very best to help Fidgety recover. She was lying listless and hardly noticing anything around her. Her mother was constantly at her side and weeping constantly. The others were trying their very best to comfort the mother, as well as help coax Fidgety to eat and drink. However, even that was becoming a tough chore as Fidgety hardly moved.

Her breathing became more and more labored. It became apparent to the whole group that the situation was desperate and that it was unlikely Fidgety will recover. The smell from the wound was becoming unbearable and copious amounts of yellow fluid were leaking from the wound. Even this did not deter her mother. She was constantly in attendance. One morning, the agony of Fidgety and the whole group was over. She was not moving. Her mother tried her best to get her to respond. No more foam escaped from Fidgety's mouth. Her mother and most of the youngsters were wailing. Nobody moved; most didn't even eat anything.

Some of the adults brought twigs and leaves and placed them over the body of Fidgety. However, there was not enough to cover her body. They did try to cover the leg with the wound completely. The smell was still unbearable. Thus, Spotty decided it was best if the group moved to a different location. Reluctantly Fidgety's mother also left her. She did walk around the listless body a few times, as if to say goodbye and stroked Fidgety's forehead with her trunk before departing. Then, she joined the others in the group. She did turn back and plant a lingering look at Fidgety, after walking some paces. The group had settled on a location far enough away from the distressing events of the past few days.

Slowly, the group returned to normal activities. It was such a relief to see kids playing again, and it was even nice to hear the grown-ups scolding the children! As usual, time helped heal the wound of the loss of Fidgety.

Chapter Four

The afternoon sun was pounding on us. Even though all of us were flapping our ears around to keep ourselves cooled down, we were all almost panting. The intense heat and the pesky flies were the real bugbears during the summer. But what were we to do? The days were long and the sun was right above our heads all the time. Nobody was in the mood to play either. We kids could tell the adults were irritable, and we daren't trouble them with anything under the circumstances.

We were in the middle of a vast field full of different types of animals. Most were grazing in the grass. There were numerous striped animals, eating, nudging, tails swaying from side to side. Their noses were flared, the ears were constantly in motion, trying to ward off the flies and other insects. There were many types of smaller animals with and without horns. All were busy munching. The violent animals were always trailing these poor beings. We hated to watch the chase and eventual demise of some of the meek animals. I always wished I could do something to stop the butchery. I hated to see blood being spilled. I had often asked my elders why such violence had to take place. And the answer was always that, without the prey animals, the violent ones would not survive. OK, but what about those babies that fall prey often? It was always heart-breaking to see them being hunted down and eaten half alive!

All those violent acts made me realize that fortunately we never had to kill any other animal to survive. No blood was spilled by us. Of course, if one analyzes this matter, we did eat grass; lots of them. And, each grass was a living thing. So, we were actually killing vastly more living things than those who kill another animal and eat it. Oh Well! There is no end to such philosophizing.

Suffice it to say that there were always activities in this field. It was like a live stage where all those cruel acts were acted out constantly. The ground would get stirred up wherever there was a chase and killing. Sometimes a surprise escape by the intended victim was a welcome sight. This afternoon, the place was relatively quiet, perhaps due to the heat. In fact, far away near the horizon one could see shimmering in the air from the intense heat. That was enough to make one depressed. That was when I would think of a good mud bath. Mmmm…

Suddenly all of us were rattled by one of our juveniles who came dashing at the group like lightning. He was coming from the small patch of trees behind us, many elephant paces away. He was puffing and panting and shaking all over. He was shaking like a leaf. And from the look in his eyes, we could tell he had experienced something terrible. Almost all of us in unison asked him (he was Jerky, the perennial worrier.)

"What's the matter?" He just couldn't talk for several moments. Panting and puffing and trying to gather his thoughts.

He stuttered "I…I…"

"What, What?" All of us again asked in unison.

"Spit it out lad." Spotty was losing patience.

"I…Uh…I saw. Oh! It's terrible." He was again stuttering. He was so agitated that he couldn't bring himself to speak coherently.

Spotty tried a different approach. "Look, lad, what are you trying to say? Don't worry about a thing. We are all here."

"You don't know…you don't know…what I saw," Jerky was panting again. He tried to gather himself.

"I…I…I saw them kill."

"Who killed who?" Spotty again…

"Oh! They are so cruel. I saw…I saw them kill…It was Rash. He…was like a brother to me."

Rash was my very best friend and confidant. He was a young male, almost fully grown and with magnificent tusks. He was called Rash as he did things in a rash (of course) on impulse. He was, however, a good lad. He never gave anybody any trouble. So everyone was distressed by what they heard. To his mother, our aunty Calm one the news came as a lightning strike; she froze. It looked as if she would collapse, but for the other grownups standing next to her. The aunts instinctively began comforting her, stroking her trunk and forehead with the tips of their trunks. They were taking turns to do this. Tears flowed from Calm one's eyes and most of the other aunts'.

By now, Jerky was somewhat settled.

He said, "I saw Rash fall after those devils blast the tube. Oh! That terrible sound." By then Jerky had regained more composure.

He continued, "Rash fell down bleeding from his head…from right here." Jerky was pointing with his trunk to the right side of his head, below the eye.

"He fell down immediately. He couldn't get up, although he tried to. Then…then…" He was agitated again. Jerky couldn't find words.

The group was more understanding by now. They waited. Jerky was still panting but could muster a few more words.

"They (the devils on two legs) closed in…they had big knives…and they started to…" He was panting again.

Jerky started to shake again. He was shaking his head from side to side conspicuously. Obviously, he was reliving the sight and having a terrible time of it.

"I saw them hack into him."

"Oh! So terrible!"

"They were hacking into him and he was crying…He was still alive! They were cutting around the tusk. My best friend! And I couldn't help. I was so afraid."

Now the group knew what Jerky had just gone through.

"So they killed him." Spotty was taking stock. "They wanted his tusks…those magnificent tusks. But they couldn't even wait until he was dead!" We could see Spotty become depressed. Her eyes were moist and she was looking down. All of us were in shock. How cruel those devils were! We elephants meant no harm to anybody. The only fault (if it can be called that) was that we grow tusks and those devils cherish them. And obviously, the better formed the tusks were, the more in danger the owner of those tusks was.

The younger members of the group jumped up and were ready to run to the scene to take revenge on the devils. Of course, the grown-ups with more experience were more cautious. They knew they couldn't match the power of the blasting tube that the devils used to kill animals. In fact, they knew they couldn't really do anything to right the wrong that was done. The whole group was in deep distress.

By now, the sun was painting the horizon in deep crimson as if to remind everyone the day was giving way to night. That was definitely not a source of comfort to the group; they knew all sorts of danger lurked after dark. Especially after the terrible news, they had just received about the fate that befell Rash. Jerky couldn't sleep that night; neither did most of the group. All the juveniles grouped together, comforting one another. The older members stroked the babies gently with the tips of their trunks. The grown-ups were pretending to be brave but all of us knew they were on edge throughout the night. No one really slept that night, at least not a restful sleep.

When we woke up, the sun was already high up in the sky and pounding on us. We noticed the elders already up and grouped together. The air was heavy with consternation; everybody was shaken so much by the news Jerky brought to the group last evening. We heard a quiet wailing coming from the group. That was Aunty Calm one again; as the name suggested, she was known for being calm and collected most of the time. But this morning she had reason to appear rattled; Rash was her only son and obviously, she was going through unbearable agony. The rest of the family was trying to calm her down. Most took turns to feel her with their trunks and gently patting on her forehead and ears. This was the first time we had ever seen Calm one actually sobbing; tears were flowing down her face. Spotty was standing close to her, rubbing her belly against hers. Obviously, everyone was trying their best to console her. However, it didn't look like their efforts were having much effect on her.

We could hear Calm one uttering something to the elders who were standing around her and comforting her. I went closer to hear what she had to say. Her voice was so muted, I had trouble hearing her but from Spotty's response, I knew she was insisting on going to where Rash was last seen by Jerky the previous evening.

"One last time, please..." she was heard pleading to Spotty. "I have to give him his last rites."

Spotty turned to the senior members as if to get their consensus but we could also get the sense that Spotty was somewhat hesitant to go to the same killing ground, in case those murderers were still there. That would put the other members of her clan at risk as well.

However, Calm one insisted on going there. As a mother, what else could she wish for? With some more coaxing, and with consensus among the elders, Spotty gave in. In the back of her mind has been the consideration that, if the group did not say farewell to Rash, his mother Calm one would suffer greatly and, we would reach a point of no return. I mean, what is the point in going to that place when we cannot even see Rash for one last time? So, the family had to make the trip now, rather than at a later date.

The group gathered all the kids and juveniles and Spotty explained to them the purpose of their trek. She also wanted to warn them about the gruesome sight they might witness when they reach there.

Spotty turned to the youngest of the group and said, "All of you know what happened, don't you? When we reach that place and find Rash, you understand he won't be able to talk to you. Right?"

Most of us nodded our heads.

"And I don't want any histrionics there, understand? Be respectful…and we, your aunts will show what you all need to do. Just follow us in order and imitate us. OK?"

When she felt that she had prepared the kids, Spotty motioned to Jerky to show the way. Thus, the whole family group began their journey. All of them knew it was not too far, from what Jerky had told them yesterday. Everyone was in a deeply somber mood; most did not even talk. They formed a line and followed Spotty and Jerky, and the other elders. Calm one was right behind the leaders. The other aunts and the older kids followed, almost according to their seniority. The babies were, of course, stationed in the middle of the formation, for their own safety. Throughout the trek Aunty Calm one was heard whimpering, tears still flowing from her eyes. She constantly fell back from the group; the sadness was bearing down on her so much. I felt so sad seeing the usually calm and collected Aunty in this pathetic state.

My family paying respects to the fallen Rash

Soon we reached a clearing beyond the cluster of trees that we were going past. We could see from a distance a faint figure of an elephant lying prostrate. There were many long-necked birds surrounding the site, some of them on top of the body and tearing into it. There were many more around the body and clearly making a ruckus, apparently fighting for the best spot. As we approached, these birds gave way but they did not go too far away. Also, as we neared the scene, the real extent of the gore became obvious. We could clearly make out that the elephant was not whole. The body was on the ground, on its tummy and we could see the forehead and ears but, beyond the point where the trunk joins the head, we could see rough edges of raw flesh. There was dried up blood all over the area. Just a pace away, we saw Rash's trunk lying on the ground. It was such a pitiable sight and so gruesome, most of us turned our heads away. Some of the juveniles and kids were retching, but no one actually vomited. One of the young females actually fainted; some of us went to attend to her. By now, we could hear Calm one crying, in a deep, low-pitched voice; she cried and cried to exhaustion. She couldn't make herself go up to the dead body of Rash, at least for now. Spotty, as usual, took the lead in going up to Rash's fallen body. First, she touched his forehead and body with the tip of her trunk and gently stroked him. She then knelt and stayed immobile for a short time; what was going through her mind is unknowable as she did not utter a word. Maybe she was praying for Rash's welfare in the 'other world' but maybe she was just grieving but did not want the youngsters to see weakness in her. Perhaps she was contemplating and re-creating the scene of the butchery of poor Rash and the agony he must have gone through. Perhaps she was considering the incredible cruelty those animals on two legs were capable of. She was heard heaving a long sigh.

Then she got up, walked around the body, making sure she did not trample his trunk. Of course, Rash's tusks were missing. Oh! Those magnificent tusks; we all knew that his life was taken simply for those well-formed, beautiful tusks. Aunt Spotty also wanted to check and make sure the body belonged to Rash, and for that, she needed another identification mark. And that was the twist on his tail and sure enough, that unique twist about the middle of his tail was indeed present.

When Spotty came back to the group and motioned to the others to do their rituals, one by one the aunts and then the others, according to their ages and seniority went forward. Some knelt down; others simply felt the forehead of Rash with the tips of their trunks. Some lingered for a while with the body. Calm one was the last to pay her respects. She was wailing fairly loud by now. She was also saying, "Oh! My poor boy. What they did to him! How could anybody do this to such a gentle boy? He meant no harm to anybody." So saying, she lay down beside him, feeling his abdomen with her trunk and gently stroking. It was so touching; most of us were in tears. She then picked up the trunk and placed it in contact with the severed neck of Rash, she lingered for some more time, and then she arose. But she couldn't tear herself away from Rash. Spotty came forward, to both console her and pull her away from Rash's body. Calm one was shaking from head to tail but did not move.

This intensely painful scene must have lingered for a very long time. I know this because by then the sun was right above us and beating hard. The younger ones among us were eager to go back to our home, where there were some shady trees. Most of us were emotionally drained, having witnessed the gory scene and obviously become aware of the incredible cruelty those horrible animals inflicted on poor Rash. We were all depressed and forlorn and were eager to get away from the murder scene. Finally Aunty Calm one was ready to part with Rash. As we started our trek back, after a few paces, Aunt Calm one looked back, a long, lingering look at the severed and mutilated body of Rash. She heaved a heavy sigh. She also sobbed all the way back home…

Chapter Five

Here I was in the middle of what can be described only as a jungle. As far as the eye could see the field was filled with all sorts of tasty plants. Especially the long sticks with succulent stems with very sweet juice. Yum…I had with me all my friends and the younger relatives. They were also having the time of their lives. In fact, all of us were running around and munching 'like there was no tomorrow'. I'd say it was more like kids in a candy store. What was even more interesting was, there were no other animals to share all this abundance of food. None of the annoying little animals that were always trying to share our food. Somehow, they seemed to like the same type of food. That was always annoying, although, we could reach higher than most other animals (with one exception, which was the animal with long necks and spots on their skin. We called them (appropriately) 'long necks'.

I didn't even spot any birds here. Where were they? I liked the small birds that would climb on my back, perch near my ears, and remove some nasty pests from inside my ears. I guess they were gone for gathering food or water. I don't know. For the very same reason, the place was very quiet. Not that I was complaining about that; it is good to have some peace and quiet sometimes. And, as long as there was enough to eat and we had good company, why complain? I also noticed there were no grownups there. Now, that was strange! Where would they have gone? In the back of my mind was a real relief in not having the adults around, because they were usually weaving rules around us the kids. So it was a nice escape for us.

All that frolicking made me somewhat careless. It was as if there was nothing in this heaven that we had to fear. That was until I spotted a long slithering animal grab my right foot. First, I didn't care too much as it wasn't painful or anything. Soon I became aware of it pulling on my leg. I tried to pull away but it didn't let go of my leg. Then I became more worried. It was not one that would bite but it was capable of strong hold. It was then twisting my leg. I couldn't free myself. And that made me nervous. I stopped eating and I called my best friend and cousin who is usually the bravest in the group, aptly called Brave lad. Now, that was strange, although I was calling him at the top of my voice and he was quite near me, he wasn't paying attention to me. He was in fact ignoring me. Of all the strange things that were happening to me, that was the strangest. I called out again. He ignored me again. The grip on my leg was annoying more. I pulled hard, saying out loud, "Go away, leave me alone." And I shook it off.

Now that is strange! I was surrounded by my cousins and other relatives. There was no lush land in sight. Instead, it was the usual landscape of parched land. And my mother Smiley was pulling on my right leg with her trunk. Oh! That was what happened! I had just wakened up. I was sleeping and having a very nice dream! I was embarrassed that I had shouted, "Go away…" All my cousins and friends had a good laugh at my expense, over this incident!

We were reminded by Spotty that we had a long way to go that day, to the mountainside. I remember the trip we took some time ago to just that spot. That was where we went to get salt. Somehow Spotty knew when we had to go to get our bodies 're-charged' with salt. It was far away and none of us looked forward to going there. But, who were we to decide? We just obeyed orders. Decision-making was the job of our elders.

The long trek began. As usual, the older members were out in front. The babies were right behind them. The juveniles and young adults trailed in the back. This kind of arrangement had another advantage; individuals of the same age group were together. To some extent that took away the monotony of such long treks.

This time, however, I had plans for something. A plan precisely for such a long trip. That was because I had developed a crush on a young cousin in our group. She was called Treasure. Yes, that was her real name. I did not mean to say she was special or something. She had the most appealing looks (to my eyes anyway). I had stolen some glances at her whenever I could but I am not even sure if she knew of my attraction to her. I was always very shy about such things and never did I gather enough courage to approach her. I would always have a big ball inside my throat when I get close to her and I had never uttered a word to her. However, I had made some plans this time.

Treasure

I walked faster to catch up with her and pretended to 'accidentally' get beside her.

I was panting, not just from the rushing but also because I was so shy and had to pluck up the courage to orchestrate the closeness to her. And, I tried to catch her attention. I was glancing through the corner of my left eye. She was walking fast, just to the left of me. If she were aware of my presence, she did not show it.

I said, "Treasure…" but no sound escaped my mouth. I tried again, "Treasure, here is something I want you to have." Again, it was no more than a whisper. She did not notice my advances.

She was, as usual, shaking her head slightly from side to side, in her gorgeous style. In fact, I had been a true secret admirer of her for quite some time. The timid me had to hide my feelings all those months.

I moved even closer to her. Now, I was almost rubbing against her. Oh! That sent shivers through my body. Here I was, in contact with the object of my desires! But she was not even noticing me.

We walked like that for some more time. Again, I plucked up enough courage to speak to her.

"Treasure."

"I have something to show you."

She looked at me, surprised. Oh! That look! How long had I waited to get her attention!

"Yes, Broken Tusk."

"What is it?"

I was overcome by shyness by now. I had a huge ball stuck in my throat, again. And, my trunk was trembling. I tried hard to hide my reaction. My heart was pounding hard. I hoped nobody was noticing my intense excitement.

That awkwardness must have gone on for a very long time. I could see Treasure eyeing me, almost teasing. Evidently, she enjoyed the attention she was receiving. And, I had always felt that the girls appear to be tougher and bolder than us, the boys. They also seem to derive pleasure in tormenting the boys. At least that was my experience. Treasure was no exception.

I plucked up courage and uttered: "Treasure, please read this…I wrote this especially for you." So saying, I produced a large leaf I had been keeping in my left ear.

"Here, this poem is my first. I hope you like it. I had been working on it for a long time." So saying, I gave her the leaf.

I was glad she didn't outright refuse to read my love song. I saw her face light up with curiosity as she took the leaf from my trunk and started to scan the poem. It read like this:

"IF I COULD…"

This solemn pledge I make to you Treasure,
If I could, I'd capture the sun in my trunk and offer;
Just to help brighten up your life my love,
And so this small token may help me prove,
My commitment, my devotion, my vow.

With these legs and trunk, I would,
Dig deep for water in desert sand dunes,
The life-giving water I bring to you love,
So that your thirst I quench, if I could.

Travel far and wide I shall without tiring,
To find you sweet fruits and twigs to your desiring,
This you can count on, just snap your trunk and I would,
No trees will stand in my way that I can't down,
I bring to thee Treasure so you may lap up,
My humble gift to you, If only I could.

Your forehead sloping gently, your tusks ever sexy,
Irresistible are your ears and body,
One couldn't sculpt a beauty truer than you,
A package is more complete and pure.
I know you notice me but scant,
With my looks, I do admit I certainly can't,

But with a heart where only love made abode,
Treasure, only now my words I found,
To commit my body, my soul to you, if I could,

If the answer is no, you'll break my heart in two,
As my heart has place Treasure, for only you;
But if it's time you need to think it through,
That's fine as waiting comes natural to me,
And eternity in love shall bind you and me.

While Treasure was reading my note, I was so shy I never looked up. I couldn't bear the thought that she might reject me. After all, I had never given her any inkling of my feelings toward her. And the wait was like all eternity.

She must have read the note at least one more time, as she seemed to have taken a long time. That was surely a good sign. She certainly didn't reject me outright.

I glanced across to find some response from her. To my surprise, she was actually sobbing.

"What did I say wrong?" I was baffled.

She just shook her head. To the two of us, there were no others present. The whole world was made of just the two of us.

"Treasure, please I did not mean to offend you. Forgive me if I upset you in some way." I couldn't understand her unexpected response.

"I just didn't know you had even noticed me," said Treasure. "That was a most moving statement. And a good piece of literary work."

"How long had you been carrying that poem in your ear?"

"Oh! Many, many days. I just had to find the 'right' time. And you know how shy I am."

"So, what do you say?" I wanted to know her answer, more than her critique of the literary merit of my poem.

Treasure was still silent. I stole glances at her while waiting for her answer but also just to look at her gorgeous person. I was certainly feeling more comfortable and I could make the statement that I was already on cloud nine. Here was the object of my desires who was seriously pondering a romantic alliance with me. Me, the mere mortal, Broken Tusk!

"There is plenty of time. Why don't we sleep on it, so to say?"

"Let's enjoy this trip for the now."

She was walking right next to me now, clutching the note I had handed her.

I said, "Why don't you keep the poem safe somewhere so you won't lose it?"

"No, this is not going anywhere," she said, "as soon as I get back, I am going to keep it with my most 'treasured' (no pun intended!) possessions."

We were now walking shoulder to shoulder, and literally rubbing our bellies together at times. Oh! That was such a sensation! Here, at last, was my heartthrob, and it looked as if she had accepted me. I found the courage to hold her sexy trunk in mine. I had the tip of my trunk kind of curled around the middle of her trunk. And she let me do that. I was in ecstasy!

Our group was gradually approaching our destination. That was a hill at the far end of the horizon. Usually, this trip would have been torture for me but not this time. I did not even know how the time flew. It was as if I didn't want to reach the destination. However, we did arrive at the site. Our elders promptly set out to dig into the side of the hill and grab bits of salty rock. The bits were then swallowed whole. We, the children and the adolescents followed their example. Of course, some of the smaller children needed help from all of us, adults and the older children.

I can't say if I enjoyed eating that stuff as it was kind of bitter and salty and the texture was definitely un-wholesome. But, we all knew this 'diet' was important for our health and we just had to put up with the taste and everything else. At least, we only had to eat this terrible stuff once in a while! I was in a group of males of roughly the same age. That also meant that for the duration of the diet, I had lost sight of Treasure. And I couldn't wait to get back together during our return trip.

Chapter Six

The seasons came and went. And nothing much new happened. Our lives followed a set plan; everything went according to a pattern set by Spotty. She fixed everything; what we do. Where we go. When we go there. And, precisely what happens when we arrive at our destinations. It was so regimentalized!

Over the last several months I had bonded well with Treasure. Although we could not say we were inseparable, more often than not, we were together. Needless to say, that inevitably invited taunting from other youngsters. Not exactly jealousy but curious looks and smiles. Sometimes we endured jokes, as well. But, we were able to brush off all of them and take everything in our stride. Until something happened. And, it had to do with Crafty. That was the juvenile known for his cunning deeds. Nobody liked him. He looked ugly, with a pockmarked tusk and torn ears and, he acted ugly. I usually left him alone. His language was filthy and he would talk bad about just about everybody. I didn't know how even his mother would have liked him. You know there are characters like him in every society; I am sure even in non-elephant societies.

One day he approached me; like, buddy, buddy. I knew instinctively that it probably meant trouble. I tried to ignore him but he touched my shoulder with his trunk.

I stopped and looked in his direction.

"Hey! B.T. (that was an abbreviation for Broken Tusk)."

He knew very well that 'B.T.' always annoyed me. I looked away and continued to walk. But Crafty was again rubbing his shoulder with me.

"Listen, Broken Tusk. I don't mean to upset you, but I have been wanting to say something to you for a while."

I said, "Yes and I know it will be trouble. But go ahead."

"Now, now. You are reading too much into it."

"Why don't you spit it out? What is it you want?"

"You are one lucky elephant."

"Now, why would you say that?"

"Look at the way Treasure is swooning all over you."

"Oh." I was not in the mood to discuss it. Certainly not with Crafty. And it was none of his business anyway.

"It's the first time I have seen Treasure so happy. Are you two going to make a family together?"

I kept quiet. Such probing questions! We were not even friends to discuss such things.

"We haven't discussed the matter yet. Do we have some time?"

I don't like to be sarcastic, but what else does this call for?

Crafty was undeterred. He lengthened his pace so he could keep up with me. Of course, I had been walking faster to get away from him. He dropped a 'bomb'.

"But I know your affair will not last."

"Now, why do you think that? Do you happen to have control over such things?"

A cunning smile crossed his face. And I was literally shaking with rage.

"I will see to it that you two become enemies soon."

I couldn't believe my ears. I said, "Let me see how you do that." I was comfortable with my relationship with Treasure and I knew no upstart elephant juvenile was going to rupture that!

Crafty said, "You'll see." And he departed.

I just couldn't bear the sight of that ugly behind of his as he trotted away. Oh! I was so angry I could cry. To think that someone would even try to hurt our relationship, purely out of spite! I also couldn't imagine how he might orchestrate that. Surely he would try to tell Treasure all sorts of lies.

I quickly located Treasure. She was unaware of all the commotion and was munching away on some leaves and twigs, with her friends. And she was rubbing her left eye with the tip of her trunk, ever so lightly. Oh! It was such a heavenly sight!

"Treasure, Treasure..." I called her. "There is something important I want to tell you."

She stopped eating. "Is it that serious?"

"You could say that. Our relationship is serious, is it not?"

"Hmm. Of course; why would you think otherwise?"

"Well, there is somebody trying to hurt our relationship."

"Who? And why?"

"Well, the who is your enemy and mine, Crafty?"

"And, as to why you should ask him. Jealousy, I suppose, or just plain meanness."

"Oh! He is capable of anything. But he is in for a surprise."

"No, Treasure. He might tell you all sorts of things about me. I don't know what he is up to. Just be alert."

"Broken Tusk. Forewarned is forearmed. You don't have to worry. This time we will hand him a defeat. That out-of-control brat!"

"Let's talk about something more pleasant." So saying, I escorted Treasure to where the group was grazing. We did not talk much as we approached them. It was mid-afternoon, and the group had been eating all morning and had settled down to simply grazing, as was their habit.

Then we became aware of some commotion coming from a little distance away. We both rushed to see what was going on. What was going on was a game we played sometimes. A game that healthy, fit, strong elephants engaged in. It was so much fun for both the players and the onlookers alike. Usually, two or three players would line up, facing an equal number of other players. Then, the two opposing players at the front of each line would grab the trunk of the other and pull hard. The players who have lined up behind these, frontline players would hold onto the tails of the respective players just in front of them. The idea was to pull hard so that the opponents are pulled over to the other side. The game was won when one side was so strong the other players crossed over to their side. Of course, it was hard work and everybody had a good workout playing this game.

I joined in at the back of one of the teams. And that left Treasure to root for me and my team. I could hear her scream, "Come on Tusk!" It was such a surprise that I could discern her screams apart from all the other noises!

"Kill them, kill them…" called out someone.

"Harder, harder," came the reply.

The pulling went seesawing. For some time, nobody could be sure who would win. You could hear the elephants panting and puffing.

There was dust kicked up all around. The elders in the group were some distance away, but they were also caught up in the action. They were also checking to make sure the game remained a sport and didn't turn foul.

"Pull, pull. Harder, harder." There was such confusion all around!

This pulling and yelling went on for what seemed like an eternity. Suddenly, out of nowhere came Trouble running toward the contestants. He went right through the clasped trunk and tail of two of the contestants, thus disrupting the game. All of them fell back and tumbled one on top of the other. The dust that kicked up! The mess Trouble made for the whole group! But no one dared take Trouble to task, as usual. He always did things like this and got away with them; his mother Spotty's position in the group guaranteed that. In any case, the game was over and neither group had won. So much for the fun that it was supposed to bring to the group.

Around the same time of the year, I remember making a journey to the watering hole with our group. The nearest river had dried up so we had to go farther to a deep well that Spotty and the other elders knew well. The group had made the formation, as usual. I made sure I was walking alongside Treasure. It looked like a long trip, not that I minded too much. In fact, journeys had become much more enjoyable with Treasure at my side. The terrain was quite familiar, with rolling meadows interspersed with trees of varying sizes. There were numerous animals foraging; some in groups and others all alone. I saw a group of very chubby animals with horns on the front of their heads. They looked formidable. There was a family of them. Everybody gave way to that group. Surprisingly, they were also eating grass and were not at all aggressive. Even so, Treasure was frightened of them.

She said, "Oh! Don't they look dangerous?"

"Those long, curled horns and the stocky build. I wouldn't want to have anything to do with them."

"But you know Treasure, they are really gentle animals, despite their looks. They don't kill animals either. Of course, they might be dangerous if we try to harm them."

"Let's give them a wide berth." So saying, Treasure went as far away as possible away from the part of the meadow where the horned beasts were situated.

"So, how has life been treating you?"

"Oh! Nothing much to brag about. I did talk to my mother about you. She really likes you and I am so relieved about that. I didn't want her to fight me about our relationship. It was interesting. She said you remind her of my father. Same looks, apparently. But, you are more handsome, right?"

She had a certain gleam in her eyes. I nodded my head. *Of course.*

Treasure was beginning to pant by now. Oh! How much I admired her looks; even when she was tired and not at her best. She had the cutest forehead and trunk and the way she swayed her head from side to side when she walked, was so adorable!

I couldn't help myself, and I said, "Treasure…"

"What?" She replied.

"I love you."

"Now, what is that for?"

"Well, how about you?"

"Of course, do I have to keep on saying it?"

I was blushing by now. Again I was in a blissful state. And there was no more need for words. We had walked for a very long time by now. Everybody was panting. The smaller children were getting fidgety. Some of the youngsters were asking, "How much longer?"

The elders had come to a stop by now. The whole group slowed down and stopped. No one was sure why.

It soon became apparent why they had stopped. On the ground, we spotted some bones, in a heap. They were white, stripped of all meat, skin, and tissues. We soon realized the bones belonged to an elephant (Although, there were no tusks, the skull and the location meant for the tusks were obvious).

"It looks like an elephant that had died recently," said one of the elders.

"Why do you think that?" Spotty wanted to know.

"Look at the nails. They do not last for more than a short time, do they?"

"Now, that's true."

Most of the elders were huddled around the skeleton, turning the bones around gently, sniffing, and then contemplating. They were careful about not disturbing the distribution of the bones. It was as if they didn't want to be disrespectful to the animal that the bones bore at one time.

"I wonder who these bones belonged to." Treasure was more or less thinking aloud. She was curious but also scared of touching those dead bones. It was as if the person who once carried them was close by.

In fact, the other juveniles just stayed away. In elephant society, death is regarded as a great mystery. No one had explained to us where they go after death. Why is it, one moment someone is active, with feelings and emotions, and another they are not there anymore? Do they ever come back? Of course, no one had come back to tell us. Are they living somewhere else, and want nothing more to do with us? Why would they do so? On the other hand, are they still around and it is just that we cannot see them?

Treasure had always been scared of the dark and of all the noises she would hear from the land. She stayed close to me, rubbing her body against me, and she held my trunk in hers. It was like she wanted reassurance. I tried to console her by gently stroking her trunk and shoulder. I could feel her shaking, and I thought to myself, *Oh! These girls. They are so flimsy.*

One of the mothers discovered the sixth toe on the right foot of the skeleton and she said out aloud, "Look at this foot! It is just like Rash's."

Spotty responded, "Why indeed, this could be Rash. Wasn't it here that he was attacked by those devils?" Her face was contorted with obvious pain.

Rash's mother was by now in tears. "Oh! How much he must have suffered. Rash, Rash won't you come back?"

She knew that of course, it was hopeless. The other elephants consoled her. They were examining the bones gently, turning them over and looking for clues. They were all certain the bones belonged to Rash. Now, in elephant custom the dead need to be respected. That called for a simple ritual of walking around the remains and chanting (ever so gently, in our low-pitched voice), "Forget all worries, you now have peace. No one can touch you now, you are in nether land."

Some of the mothers brought twigs to place beside Rash's bones. Some placed stones next to him. It was like the place was being marked. Then it was time to leave.

Spotty started to walk. And slowly the others followed. Only Rash's mother did not move. Tears were flowing from her eyes. She was moving her head from side to side, in a despondent manner. And she couldn't find the energy to get up.

Noticing this, Spotty stopped and the others stopped as well. They wanted to give Rash's mother more time.

Finally, she was ready. She gently stroked all the bones with her trunk. She whispered, "Rash, I miss you so much. How I wish I could bring you back, my son. I am so lonely now, and I don't know how much more I can bear."

She got up and started to walk. She must have taken just a few paces and she looked back. Then she stopped. It was as if she didn't want to leave Rash's bones. Her maternal instincts were really at work. It was like she had to be there to take care of him. This went on for what seemed like a long time. Spotty showed great restraint and compassion. She stayed put until Rash's mother was ready to leave.

Everyone was aware of the weight of the moment. No one talked. Even the kids were understanding. There were some others also in tears. All of us were thinking about the last moments of Rash and the terrible suffering he had gone through.

Reluctantly, Rash's mother also left the bones and joined the group on their journey. With heavy hearts and renewed kinship, all the members of the group moved away. Although there were no definite landmarks, many knew they could remember the spot the next time they went this way.

Spotty indicated that they would return home. She didn't want the group to travel anymore, with the weight of the discovery they had made.

Chapter Seven

It was a very hot morning and I was already struggling to breathe. I fanned my ears hard to cool them. So were all the others. Oh! This heat wave! I looked across the savannah. There were lots of other animals as well, and they were all in pretty much the same situation. All were trying to be in the shade or were wagging their tails trying to get rid of the pests. The land was shimmering and making the images flutter and dance in the intense heat.

"Hello, B.K."

I immediately knew who that was. Who else will annoy me with my initials? That was Crafty, of course. I thought to myself, *Now what disaster could he have for me?*

"What do you want now?"

"Now, now. Don't be edgy. I am not the bearer of just bad news. I want to tell you something."

I said nothing.

"I have an important report to give you." Crafty had a decidedly wicked look on his face. And I absolutely resent that look on anybody.

"Why don't you just leave me alone?" I did not look up at him. I didn't want to see that ugly face.

"But Broken Tusk, just hear me out. You will like what you hear."

I was silent for a while. I considered the suggestion and, more to get him out of my sight and curiosity than any real need to hear his words, I said, "Spit it out. And hurry up. I don't have all day."

"OK. I'll make it short. I have a cute pet name and I am trying to let everyone know."

"Go on, what is it? Not that I am so curious to know."

"OK. It goes like this…" Crafty was really playing on my nerves. Just what you would expect from him.

"You know, I have already told some of my friends and my cousins." Then he paused again.

I said nothing. I was munching on the shrubs. It was fast approaching nightfall and I hadn't had enough to eat. I had no time to waste; especially on a jerk like Crafty. Several moments went past.

"Well, fortunately, even if I didn't tell you, I am sure you would hear it from your friend." Crafty had a strange expression plastered on his face. He had this ugliest smirk but also a wicked expression. It was hard to describe that expression.

I said, "What do you mean? You have told everyone else? And you find it hard to tell me?"

"No, that's not it. I know you will have the pleasure of learning anything bad about me. Why don't you find out from your dear friend?"

"Oh, you have already told even Treasure?"

Crafty nodded. Oh! How much I hate the sight of him!

I said, "Are you done?"

Then I walked away. I couldn't wait to get away from the stifling atmosphere. I wasn't sure if I wanted to really find out what his stupid other name was. He has annoyed me so much, I didn't really care. Why did he come all the way and engage me in this conversation? If he didn't want to tell me, why did he come out of his way to inform me of the 'new' name? Was he just here to annoy me or did he have some tricks up his trunk? I was fuming and I was in no mood to do anything, including eating. I just wanted to be alone and walked away from the group. I then lay down. I wanted to do some thinking. Of course, I was physically exhausted from the heat as well as mentally exhausted from talking to Crafty.

The next several days were spent without much excitement. Our group always followed a set pattern of activities and I can only guess that this pattern developed around Spotty's likes and dislikes. The games we played were largely left to us, except that all the grown-ups, including Spotty, kept 'an eye' on our activities so that we did not go overboard. They were always on the lookout for rough play by the larger juveniles and especially when they involved smaller kids.

One game most of us liked was dousing fine dust all over the body; most of the time we sprayed it on ourselves but often we also sprayed it on other elephants. The commotion this would cause is indescribable. There would be laughter all over with youngsters all running round, making a lot of noise. This harmless activity also had an important function; we all needed to rid ourselves of ticks and other pests. The fine dusty mud did that quite well.

What was we the youngsters making this useful activity a very enjoyable one as well?

Wrestling was another game everyone enjoyed including those who participated and those who simply watched and observed. Only, not everyone could actually wrestle. Size obviously mattered. I had done some of the wrestling but I cannot say with confidence that I enjoyed this particular activity. However, it certainly provided some diversion and also some needed exercise.

Chapter Eight

My family starting their migration

It was time for our group to move on. Something told Spotty we had to abandon our home. It wasn't just that food and water had become scarce here, or a certain wanderlust our kind has always had overcame us. Call it instinct or self-preservation. But when the time arrived, Spotty told us clearly, in her authoritarian way, "Get ready, we have a long way to go. There is no time to waste."

The kids were rummaging as usual. And the juveniles were playing games of 'who is stronger'. However, all the adults were ready. And they were in charge of herding their own children. Some called out to the youngsters; others actually restrained them. The idea was to have each family remain together as a unit but to keep the youngsters herded toward the center. This would both stop the wandering urge of the youngsters and help protect them in case of threats from other animals. One could call it a moving forest!

Then the marching order was given by Spotty. Starting slowly, the group gathered momentum. As always, in such travels in large groups, the pace was dictated by the youngest member. The mothers and other older relatives constantly kept in touch with the children using their trunks, ears, and contact with their bodies. The smell was of course the best way to know the identity of an individual. I knew each member of our group by their distinctive smell. So, using touch, smell, sight, and verbal contact, usually, the adults were able to keep the youngsters in line.

Before we knew it, we had covered much terrain. The vast expanse of dry land with an occasional tree gave way to a much more parched land. Some of the youngsters started to question, "Why are we coming to this desolate area?" In effect, they were questioning the knowledge of Spotty.

Spotty just shrugged off the doubters as if to say, "I know what I'm doing. Just wait and see." Because she was the most experienced member of our group and had the knowledge accumulated from many such travels, the adults knew not to question her. They nodded in agreement and kept the group in order. We kept moving—stomping feet, bobbing heads, waving ears and tails. To an outsider, this whole scene could have been a strange show!

Mother Gentle and Baby Fluff

We noticed Fluff slowing down (Fluff was the nickname given to the newest member of the group, by the other youngsters), and his mother Gentle slowed down to keep in step with him. The whole group slowed down just trying to keep the formation. And, once the group came to a halt. But not for long. Spotty insisted, "We cannot afford to lose time. There is still a long way to go before nightfall." The group was marching along again. But Fluff was getting really tired. He was puffing and panting. Gentle slowed down as well. Soon they were isolated. The group was moving forward and now there was some distance between those two and the rest of the group.

It wasn't long before I noticed that Gentle was rushing to keep up with the group. That meant she had decided to abandon Fluff to his fate. Now, that was sad. How is he to fend for himself? He was too young and too tired. And he must have been very frightened with Gentle now gone. I looked back and saw Fluff almost standing still. He had a sad and frightened look on his face. To me it was unbearable. So one can only imagine what emotional turmoil Gentle was going through.

Now, Gentle looked back, almost fifty paces from Fluff, with a long, contemplative type of look. I could see her eyes welling up. She stopped for a second. It was obvious she was considering her options. If she left Fluff to his fate, he was sure to perish. On the other hand, even if she was with Fluff, they could both perish without the benefit of the whole group. Then again, if Fluff had her mom with him, there was a slim chance both of them could survive. She did not have the benefit of counsel from Spotty, as she was at the head of the group and some distance away. She took a while to decide. It must have seemed like an eternity to her. She called out to Spotty, "Mother, I have to try to save my boy, if you give me permission." Spotty called out, "This is not the first time this has happened. I'll be…all of us will be sad to lose you both." I could sense a tremble in Spotty's voice. Being the matriarch, she had the responsibility of looking after the welfare of all her family, even if the decision meant losing one or two individuals in the course of a long migration.

The group plodded on. All of us kept looking back to see how Gentle and Fluff were doing. They were getting farther and farther from our group. After some more paces, they were just distant images. Seen through the dust and shimmer of the horizon the poor creatures appeared almost ghost-like. Isn't it ironic? They might well end up dead, and they were already looking as if they had already died?

We came to a shallow river and started to cross it. Spotty said to the group, "We are near our destination. Keep moving." The river was almost dry. The water came up to only a short distance from our feet. The youngest members tried to frolic in the water. All of us had a good drink of water and quenched our thirst. After lingering in this welcome cooling environment, we crossed to the other side of the river. Then more walking. We returned to our formation, with young members in the middle and the grown-ups as guardians around the outside. Ears were flapping, heads bobbing and tails wagging. Spotty told us we were almost at the destination. Were we relieved!! At last, our long-suffering feet would get some rest. Some of us did some 'dance-trotting'. This is when we pick up the front and back legs of one side at the same time. So, alternatively, the body would bob up and down. Left up, right down. Right up, left down, and so on. Although they themselves didn't participate, the grown-ups let us do it as all of us were rejoicing.

Finally, we were there. It was a really lush green area, with lots of shrubs and trees. Now we could eat all we wanted. This is why Spotty brought us here. Back where we came from the leaves were scarce and there was almost no water. So all of us started to eat in earnest. Spotty told us that this would be our home for some time to come. Needless to say, we were only too happy to know that. Now we could continue with our usual antics, only in a new location. Since wherever we were, we elephants were at the top of the pecking order, it didn't matter where we decided to make home.

Able and I playing 'Twist and Pull'

I started playing 'twist and pull' with my best friend, Able. Twist and pull is the game in which we face each other and wrap our trunks around upwards. We pull toward each other until our trunks are fairly taut and start twisting the trunks. Then we let go and start over. We do not intend to hurt each other, we are just feeling each other in a friendly way. Of course, we can only play this game with friends and when in a good mood. Otherwise, it can get serious and injuries may result. In the game, as we normally play, there are no winners or losers. Just good comradery. We usually change stances; often this results in moving around in circles. Thus, the game can go on for a long time and stop when one of the players or both get tired or bored. Occasionally, we may change partners when one retires but the other wishes to continue.

Our play was interrupted by Spotty, who called me aside, saying.

"Broken Tusk, I have an important job for you. Can you and a couple of strong boys go find Gentle and her baby Fluff? They are in great trouble…I just received her distress call."

"I'll want Brave Lad and…Able." Spotty agreed. She called the two strong young boys to her side.

"Run, boys. Gentle's and her son Fluff's safety are in your trunks. Go as quickly as you can. Run…run."

The task we were entrusted with was urgent and noble but also novel to the three of us. We had never had to go on a rescue mission. That too, with no prior knowledge of what the emergency was and therefore, what to expect. That said, the two guys that I have with me were super-duper. Well-built and strong, and also full of common sense. Brave one also had two very big tusks, quite intimidating! I could rely on both of them for facing any eventuality. After all, what sort of emergency could Gentle and Fluff be facing that the three of us could not together solve? Besides, the sense of adventure and the possibility of bringing closure to a serious and possibly disastrous situation was definitely exhilarating.

We set off immediately, on the double! Until we started to puff and pant. We then had to slow down, but because of the seriousness of the situation, we were obliged to move fast, even when we were walking. It was a real spectacle. Three male elephants in their youth, trumpeting and waving their ears wildly, kicking up dust. Our family soon disappeared behind the horizon. Suddenly, we realized we didn't even know exactly where Gentle and Fluff were. We had a very short briefing from the matriarch Spotty…She did tell us to look for the mountain with the top cut off. That is when we would see the stream, which we had to cross. Then we would find the patch of forested terrain. Beyond that, we had no clue where to search.

"How do we make contact with them?" Brave Lad was thinking aloud.

"Well, how about trumpeting loud. Then they can trumpet back."

Able was stating the obvious. Before I could respond, he was trumpeting…Loud. We both joined in the trumpeting. And then we listened.

A considerable time passed before we tried again. Then we listened again. The animals and birds that were in the neighborhood stood and listened as well. All of them must have been startled by the spectacle and the noise. You could see that they were afraid. What else can one expect after being confronted by three young bull elephants shouting on the top of their trunks?

"This isn't working." I was showing my obvious frustration. "Now what do we do?" I turned to Brave Lad.

"Listen…do you hear something?" Brave Lad had the right idea.

We stopped trumpeting. Able and I turned to Brave lad as if to ask, "What do you hear?"

"These are distress calls, for sure."

"Listen carefully." Brave lad was all ears. We also joined in to listen intently. We knew that the calls would come in the form of low-pitched noises that can only be described as 'moans'. Since such low-pitched sounds travel long distances, we elephants have been able to communicate with one another through this means for a very long time.

"It doesn't take a genius to make out this SOS. What else can these moans mean?"

"If only we could get Aunt Gentle to guide us to where they are." Brave lad was looking at the practical side. He tried pointing his ears and at the same time bobbing his head around. This was his way of 'homing in' on the source of the SOS. I couldn't join him as I couldn't hear a thing.

"I think they are coming from there." Brave lad pointed with his trunk. He still had his ears pointed and listening very carefully. Only, now he is not bobbing his head. In other words, he was sure he had determined from which direction the sounds were coming.

The group wasted no time in following their lead, although all the way to the horizon we could not find any sign of elephants. Now all three were sprinting. There was no time to waste. Whatever was happening to Gentle and Fluff, we were sure it was serious. Also, we did not want to face Spotty with our mission not accomplished. Our mission was to rescue the mother and baby.

We reached the horizon and still, there was no sign of Gentle and Fluff. Frustration was written all over these young elephants' eyes. All along, Brave Lad had been listening in.

"I think the messages are getting closer." He ushered in a sense of hope. He was looking in the direction where he felt the sounds were coming from.

"Let's go in that direction," I suggested. We were using Brave's great hearing and instincts to help us navigate. We quickened our paces. Running, puffing, and panting…

Before long, Brave lad began nodding his head.

"What is it, Lad?" I asked instinctively. Nodding is not natural for us elephants.

"Yes, I am right about the direction, and, I can hear her more clearly now." This meant that we were also getting closer to where they were.

In this commotion, we had forgotten about finding things to eat. We were the very picture of sense of purpose. And we had no time to waste. Our task meant that we get to them as quickly as possible. We could worry about hunger later.

"Don't you hear them?" Brave Lad asked us.

"Let us try. Your hearing is much more acute, lad." That was Able. Both of us tried again. The ears were pointed in the direction that Lad told us he was hearing messages.

It was not long before both of us also felt as if we were hearing Gentle's cries.

"Yes, and they sound desperate," exclaimed Able. "But she does not say what the problem is."

"Do you have any plans for what we do once we locate them?" asked the brave one.

"Well, what can we plan, if we don't know what the problem is?"

"Listen."

"She sounds much closer."

Brave Lad was now running faster. He was such a pretty picture! The tail held high, the head bobbing more wildly from side to side and the trunk sniffing constantly. Of course, the ears were the main homing in device.

Gentle's wailings were now audible to me and Able. And she seemed to be saying something like, "They are killing Fluff." Who the 'they' were not at all clear. However, we expected the worst. Some large wild animals were our first suspects. A pack of such animals could surely do great harm to a baby like Fluff. And, Gentle by herself would be no match to a large group of them. In fact, her own safety might be in jeopardy. What a terrible state they both must be in!

We must be running straight to where the mother and baby were, because, her calls were louder and more distinct. We were so encouraged that all three of us were now sprinting.

Before long, we saw Aunt Gentle. Against the setting sun, her large frame was unmistakable. No other details were discernible. Of course, Baby Fluff was too small to spot from that distance. There was a great deal of dust in the area, and that must be hiding both Fluff and his tormentors.

As we neared the location, it became clear what kind of danger the two were facing. There were no big animals, as we had suspected earlier. Instead, we saw small, dark animals in a large pack. They had surrounded the mother and the baby. The baby was tucked under the tummy of Gentle.

Before we reached the site, all three of us announced our arrival. Of course, that meant trumpeting. We were trumpeting at the top of our voices. That was enough to get the attention of the animals. They turned in our direction. By now, we were surrounding the group and the mother and baby.

Plucking up courage, with the presence of the three strong elephants, Gentle picked up one of the animals and threw it toward me. We in turn charged the group. Each of us picked up an animal, twirled it around, and tossed it high up in the air. We also gored a few of them and then stomped on their heads. There was blood everywhere.

Brave Lad and I dealing with the pesky animals

What was amazing to us was that these small animals were not at all afraid of us. They kept on charging. Of course, they had the number advantage. They also had sharp teeth and strong bites. Even with our thick hides, we could still feel the sting of their bites. And it was a battle to the finish until all of them were dead or we gave up.

We had no intention of withdrawing. There was only one outcome that was acceptable to us—outright victory and saving the mother and baby. This standoff must have gone on for quite some time. The animals were grimacing and making loud noises…barking and howling. Froth was issuing from their mouths. What a despicable picture they presented!

Brave Lad was having the time of his life! With his large tusks, he gored several of the animals to death. It looked like he was enjoying every instant of this encounter. Able was doing his bit. His technique was to toss the animals into the air and then kick them hard so that they landed far away. Those animals were so traumatized, they fled. The gory scene that all these activities presented was something to behold! There was blood all over. When the skulls were crushed by our trampling, or when the ribs or the spine were crushed by stomping on the animals, loud explosions took place and blood and tissue splashed all over. I was feeling kind of faint at the sight of all that gore and blood. I was also feeling nauseated. My tactic was changed to try to scare the animals so that they would flee and leave Gentle and Fluff alone. But then again, the way they had tormented the two very congenial elephants was totally unwarranted. And the only way to extricate the two victims from these aggressive animals was through this show of force.

Soon, the number of animals dwindled. There was a sense of relief in the air. We knew we were winning. It was just a matter of time and we will either drive away these terrible animals or kill all of them.

Now I could see the damage that had been done to our little Fluff. He looked so traumatized by all the terrible things that happened, I was not sure if he would ever recover from the shock. As I approached him, I could see that he was shaking wildly, all over. He had soiled himself as well. There were bite marks on his trunk and legs. He was bleeding from the wounds. Both he and his mother were sobbing uncontrollably. The three of us tried our best to comfort them. We were gently stroking them with our trunks while we stayed guard over them, they experienced a measure of solace.

"Aunt Gentle, time to take the trip back to Aunt Spotty and our group." I was stating the obvious. At the same time, I wasn't sure they had the energy to make the long trek. "We need to find something to eat and drink," I was considering our options in my mind. (The practical me, of course.)

As we started to walk back we noticed Fluff limping badly. He could hardly move, without buckling down on his legs. He was extremely weak, possibly from bleeding and the ordeal but it was obvious that his injuries made him very unsteady on his legs. Clearly, he needed help.

Brave Lad came up with the plan to transport Fluff. He offered to carry him between his trunk and his huge tusks. This is very rarely done (for obvious reasons) but Brave is big and strong, and we all felt that that was a viable option. Both Able and I offered to help him out if and when Brave got tired.

Thus, we set off in a formation. I led the pack. Behind me was Brave Lad carrying Fluff. Close behind them was Aunt Gentle. A few paces behind followed Able. Obviously, it was a slow trek. We also were on the lookout for some good food to eat and to get some drink. On our way over, we had crossed a stream, but that was quite far away. Near that stream, there was also some lush vegetation. That is where we needed to go. With that target in mind, we plodded on.

Fluff was moaning constantly. And Aunt Gentle was crying all the while. Tears were running down her face. Clearly, she had been re-living the terrible tragedy the two of them went through.

"Tusk." The aunt reached forward and pulled on my tail. "Why don't we send a message to Spotty that we are safe and we are on our way back?" I agreed. However, my hearing was never good. Brave lad is the best person to do the message-sending. However, since he was busy with the baby, we turned to Able. It took a few attempts by Able to get through to Aunt Spotty. Finally, when he got through, there was such jubilation from the other end; all of us could hear them.

I looked back to see how Fluff was doing. By now, he had stopped moaning. In fact, he had dozed off. Clearly, he was completely relaxed.

Soon, the terrain began to appear more familiar. We knew we were nearing the watering hole (the stream, really). Aunt Gentle said she could smell the water. That meant we were quite close to the stream.

"Do you need relief Lad?" I asked. Although he was struggling, he shook his head.

"Besides, how can you help, with your 'broken tusk'?" He was clearly enjoying the pun.

I didn't say anything. We could by now see the stream right near the horizon. We picked up the pace. Clearly, all of us were thirsty and hungry. No telling how bad both Gentle and Fluff felt.

Soon we were at the stream. With a long heave, Brave Lad let Fluff gently down. Fluff promptly lay down on the ground.

"Don't you want to drink? And eat?" His mother tried to coax him onto his feet. He shook his head. Clearly, he hadn't the strength to do anything.

Aunt Gentle found the way. She approached the stream and sucked up a trunk-full of water. Then, she returned and poured the water into Fluff's mouth. That was a long and tender moment. We, the boys were touched by that tenderness between the mother and her baby. We were near tears, but all three of us tried to hide them. Gentle went through the routine a few times. Alternately she fed Fluff water and doused his small body with it. The treatment must have re-energized Fluff. He was shaking his ears with more vigor. His wounds must also have felt some comfort from the cold water.

All of us had our fill of the water. Oh! How sweet it tasted! There is nothing like a drink or two of cold water when you are thirsty and tired. We also found enough leaves and bark to eat. Thus, satisfied, we settled down to rest. We knew we had no time to waste but we did desperately need rest…what with the battle we had gone through and the long trek (both up and down the trail).

Before long, it was time to move again. Aunt Gentle was the first to get up. She woke us boys, and soon we were ready.

Able offered to carry Fluff for the rest of the trip, and Brave Lad agreed. Able didn't have the long, strong tusks like Lad, but he was also a big, strong elephant. In fact, he didn't have much trouble either, in carrying baby Fluff. Now he was right behind me. Brave Lad stayed at the back of the pack. He was indeed the right one to guard the rear of the group!

We were in touch with Aunty Spotty and the group constantly, and we could sense that they were getting nearer and nearer. Aunt Gentle couldn't contain herself at the thought of joining her matriarch and her family. She came close to losing her precious son and perhaps even losing her own life at the hands of those terrible animals!

Soon we could see the group at the far end of the field. And we could hear the trumpeting and jubilation coming from the youngsters in the group. We were almost running by now; and many of our family members came forward as well, to greet the mother and baby. The tenderness of the moment was palpable. There was dust everywhere made by the stomping and running of this large group of elephants. Soon they were embracing us; the trunks were intertwined, the bellies rubbing one another. Stealthily I slipped away and found my love. And a sweet embrace followed. I could see a stream of tears coming down her luscious cheeks. I rubbed them off with the tip of my trunk. Treasure managed to utter these beautiful words, between her sobbing, "Broken Tusk, you did it!" What a wonderful gift she managed to give me with those five words!